Barbie as The Island Princess

A TRUE PRINCESS

Based on the original screenplay by Cliff Ruby & Elana Lesser
Interior illllustrated by SARL AKY-AKA créations

Special thanks to Vicki Jaeger, Monica Okazaki, Rob Hudnut, Shelley Dvi-Vardhana, Jesyca C. Durchin, Jennifer Twiner McCarron, Shea Wageman, Sharan Wood, Trevor Wyatt, Greg Richardson, Sean Newton, Shaun Martens, Derek Toye, Sheila Turner, and Walter P. Martishius

A GOLDEN BOOK • NEW YORK

Published in the United States by Golden Books, an imprint of Random House Children's Books, a division of Random House, Inc., New York, and in Canada by Random House of Canada Limited, Toronto. Golden Books, A Golden Book, and the G colophon are registered trademarks of Random House, Inc.
ISBN: 978-0-375-84467-6   www.randomhouse.com/kids
Printed in the United States of America   10 9 8 7 6 5 4 3 2 1

A long time ago, a young girl was lost at sea.

During a storm, the girl fell overboard and was rescued by dolphins.

Help the dolphins get to the island.

FINISH

START

The next day, Azul the peacock and Sagi the red panda found the girl's trunk, which had washed ashore on the beautiful island.

Sagi and Azul also found the girl and decided to take care of her . . .

. . . as she grew up on the island. Her name was Ro.

One day, a ship of sailors discovers the island.

Help the sailors get to the island.

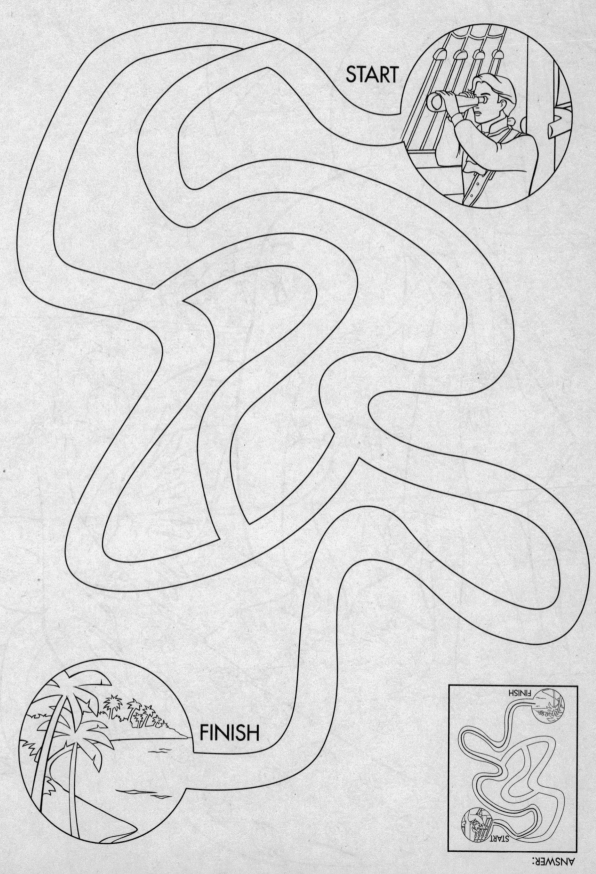

START

FINISH

ANSWER:

Ro and her animal friends sneak a peek at the ship.

Prince Antonio is one of the sailors. He and his friend
Frazer begin to explore the island.

Can you find 5 differences between this page and the opposite page? Circle them.

ANSWER: On this page, the butterfly's wings are different; a palm tree is missing; the flowers on the vine are missing; the leaves in front of Prince Antonio are different; and Frazer's bag is missing.

Since Ro has grown up among animals,
she doesn't remember having seen another person.

While exploring, Prince Antonio and Frazer
slip and begin to slide!

Some crocodiles start to attack the two men, but Ro comes to their rescue.

"No eating the guests, Fang!" says Ro.

"Who are you?" asks Prince Antonio.
"Who are you?" asks Ro.

Ro tells the prince how she came to be on the island. She shows him her trunk, which has *RO* on it.
The letters explain why she thinks her name is Ro.

Trace the letters of Ro's name.

Ro tells the prince that she doesn't remember anything about her past. All she knows is she came from the sea.

Frazer introduces the young man as Antonio,
Prince of Appolonia.

The prince offers to take Ro back to his kingdom, but she isn't sure what do to. Her home is on the island!

Ro starts to wonder about where she came from.
Connect the dots to see the night sky.

Ro goes with the prince, and she brings her
animal family along.

As they sail toward Appolonia, Prince Antonio and Ro
begin to fall in love.

Tika worries that if Ro falls in love with the prince, she might leave her animal family behind!

When they reach the prince's land, Ro can't believe her eyes.
"Everybody's like me!" she exclaims.
"But nobody's like me," says Tika, who wants to go home.

The prince is taking Ro to the castle and wants her to ride in a carriage with him. Ro decides to ride on Tika instead.

No one can believe that a girl would rather ride with animals than in the prince's carriage!

Once Prince Antonio reaches the castle, his sisters, Princesses Rita, Sofia, and Gina welcome him home.

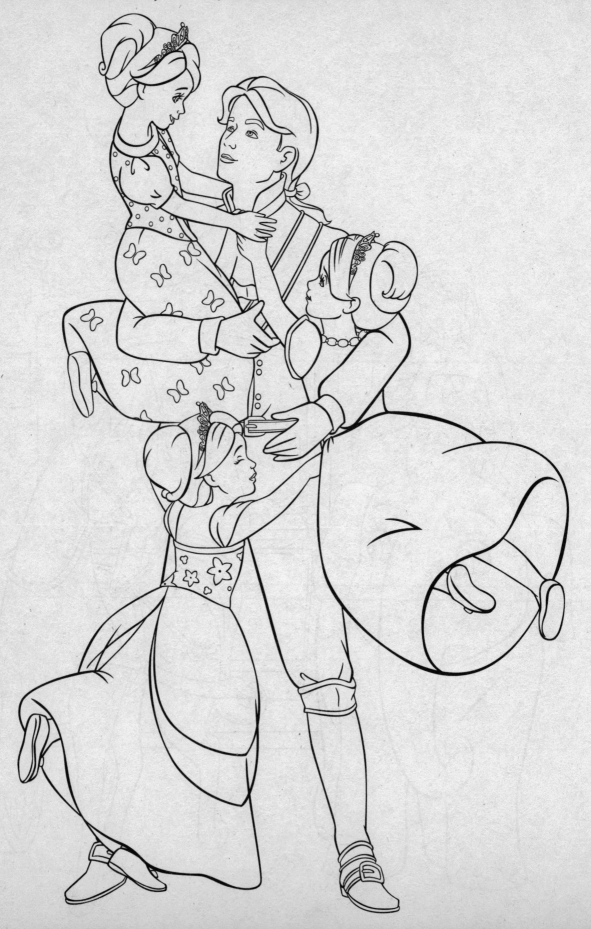

"Is this your pet?" asks Princess Sofia.
"No, Tika is part of my family," says Ro.

Azul introduces himself as Prince Azul, but only Ro can understand him.

Use the key to color Azul's beautiful feathers!

KEY

1 = blue   2 = green   3 = purple   4 = red   5 = yellow

The prince can't wait for Ro to meet his parents!

While Prince Antonio was away, his father, King Peter, decided that his son should marry a princess named Luciana. Antonio's mother, Queen Danielle, isn't so sure about the marriage.

Prince Antonio introduces Ro to his mother and father.
He tells them about finding her on an island.

Ro talks to Tallulah, the queen's monkey, but all the king and queen hear is chattering. The king doesn't know what to think about Ro talking to an animal.

Finally, the king tells Prince Antonio about the wedding plans he has made. The prince is shocked.

Then Prince Antonio meets Luciana's mother,
Queen Ariana.

Prince Antonio tells his parents he doesn't want to marry
Luciana because he loves Ro. But they tell him he has to
marry a princess.

Ro begins to have second thoughts about leaving the island. She sees that she doesn't fit in with everyone else.

Luciana isn't sure if she should marry Prince Antonio. She wants to marry someone who really loves her, but her mother has other ideas.

Long ago, Queen Ariana's family had tried to kill King Peter, and he took their land to punish them. Now Ariana wants to get back at him by having Luciana marry Prince Antonio. Then she can rule the kingdom through her daughter!

The next day, Ro has tea with the royal family. But she doesn't know how to hold her teacup. Prince Antonio's parents think she is very strange.

Ariana trips the butler to make him spill food on Ro.
Luciana, who is not mean like her mother, tries to help
Ro clean off her clothes.

Ro feels a bit sad and sings a song she remembers from her childhood.

Use the key to color the garden flowers!

KEY

| 1 = red | 2 = green | 3 = pink |

Tallulah has been living at the palace for so long, she has forgotten what it is like to be a wild monkey. Ro shows Tallulah how to eat without a knife and how to swing through the trees!

The king doesn't want his son to marry Ro—a girl who
swings through the trees like a monkey! He admits that
Queen Ariana isn't nice, but Luciana is very kind.
The king tells the prince that he MUST marry Luciana.

As the wedding plans continue, Princess Sofia dresses
Tika for the engagement ball.

The animals help Ro get ready for the ball.

Help Ro get ready for the ball! Color her dress.

The animals work together to make Ro look beautiful.

At the ball, Princesses Rita, Sofia, and Gina are having
a wonderful time.

Princess Luciana and Prince Antonio talk and dance. They discover they don't really like the same things. Luciana loves the arts, and Antonio loves the outdoors.

Suddenly, Ro arrives. Prince Antonio can't take his eyes off her.

Ro doesn't know how to dance, so Prince Antonio
takes the lead.

Tallulah, Azul, and Tika are thrilled to see Ro so happy.

Circle the two pictures that match.

A

B

C

D

Meanwhile, Sagi sees a flag with a rose that he thinks he has seen before. He decides to take a closer look.

Ariana doesn't like that Ro is dancing with Prince Antonio.
She tells the king and queen that Prince Antonio and her
daughter should be married very soon.

Princess Luciana sees that Ro and the prince are in love.

Even though Ro loves Antonio, she doesn't want to hurt
Luciana. She tells him she shouldn't have come to the ball.

Sagi shows Ro the flag with the rose. He tells her that he and Azul found a flag that looked just like it the day they found her on the island.

Connect the dots to see the Paladian flag!

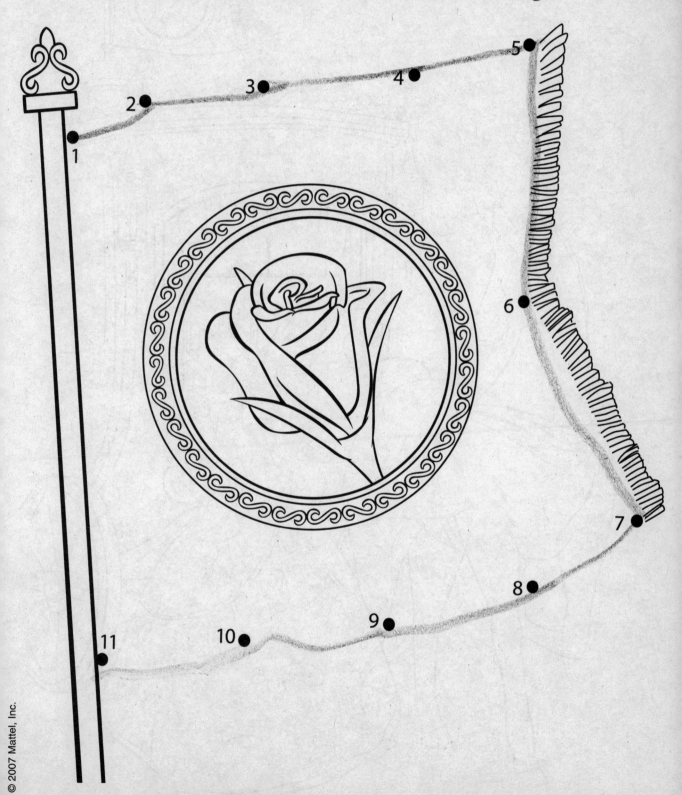

Ro asks the horse where he and the flag are from.
The horse says they are from Paladia, a nearby kingdom.
Ro wonders if she could be from there, too.

Ro leaves and tells Sagi she doesn't know where she belongs anymore.

Prince Antonio is very upset with his father and tells him he would rather give up his crown than marry someone he doesn't love.

Prince Antonio decides to go against his father's wishes.
He leaves a note for Ro asking her to sail away with him.

Tika doesn't want the prince to take Ro away from her, so she hides the note.

Help her find a good hiding place!

START

FINISH

Ariana has a plan to get rid of Ro. She gives a pouch of sleeping dust to her rats and tells them to sprinkle it on the food of all the animals in the kingdom. Then Ro and her animals will be blamed!

Tallulah drinks some milk with the sleeping dust in it and falls into a deep sleep.

Prince Antonio waits for Ro, but because she never got the note, she doesn't know he is waiting for her! He thinks she doesn't love him.

When Ro hears about what is happening to the animals, she wants to tell Prince Antonio that she thinks she can help, but the butler won't let her in!

Ariana tells Frazer that she thinks something new to the kingdom must have made all the animals sick. Frazer thinks she is talking about Ro's animals, and he tells the king and queen.

The guards put Ro and her animal family in jail!

The king agrees to free Ro from prison if Prince Antonio takes back his crown and marries Luciana.

The king arranges for Ro to be shipped back home.
Meanwhile, Ariana tells one of the sailors to make sure
Ro doesn't make it to the island.

Azul has been poisoned, too. If he doesn't wake up soon, he could be in real danger! Ro decides she will sneak back to the palace to get the medicine she knows is there.

While Ro is trying to escape, the sailor Ariana spoke to throws Sagi overboard. Ro and the rest of the animals follow and are swept out to sea!

Ro and the animals try to stay afloat! Suddenly, Ro remembers the last time she was thrown overboard, when she was a child. She remembers her father calling her name!

Use the code to find out Ro's real name.

= R = A = L

= S = O = E

_____ _____ _____ _____ _____ _____ _____

ANSWER: Rosella.

After some dolphins carry them back to shore, Tika tells Ro that she hid the prince's note because she didn't want Ro to leave her. Ro tells Tika she will always be her family and will never leave her.

It is Luciana's wedding day at the palace. Queen Marissa of Paladia arrives for the celebration.

Ariana tells her daughter not to eat any cake because it is bad luck.

But the real reason Ariana doesn't want her daughter eating
the cake is she has poured sleeping dust all over it!
A small bird sees everything and goes to tell Ro.

Connect the dots to see the cake!

Ro prepares the medicine for the sleeping sickness with island roses and coconuts.

Count how many island roses and coconuts Ro needs to make the medicine.

_____ roses

_____ coconuts

ANSWER: 3 roses and 2 coconuts.

Some guards find Ro and try to arrest her! Ro quickly
hands the medicine to Sagi and tells him to try it
on Tallulah.

Help Sagi get the medicine to Tallulah!

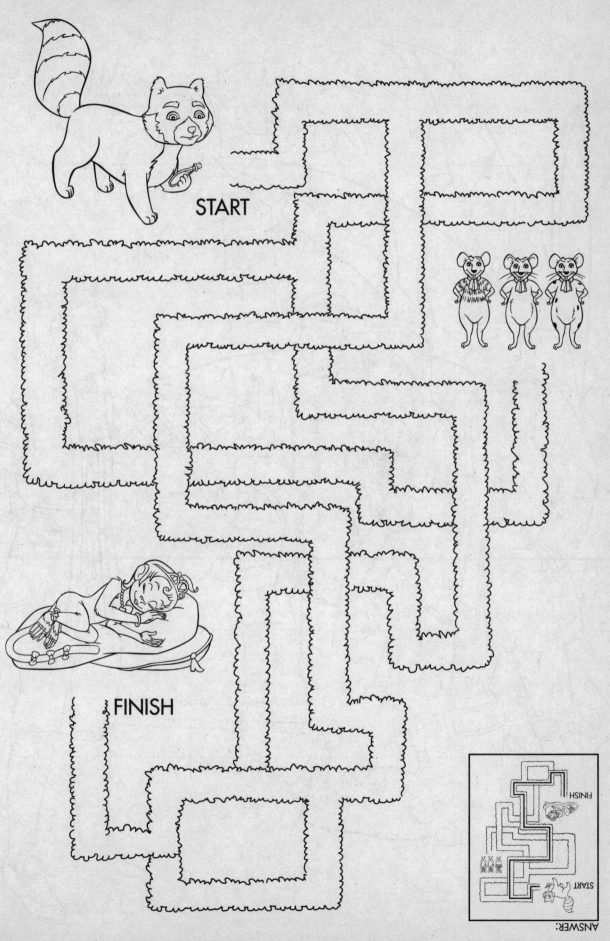

START

FINISH

ANSWER:

"Release her at once!" says Prince Antonio.

Ro explains that Ariana poisoned the animals and the wedding cake so that everyone would fall asleep after Luciana married the prince. Then Ariana could rule through her daughter, the new queen. Queen Danielle believes Ro because Tallulah is cured!

"I never wanted to hurt you," says Prince Antonio.
"I forgive you," says Luciana. "Someday someone will
look at me the way you look at Ro."

Prince Antonio asks Ro to marry him.
"Yes!" Ro says. "Yes, yes, yes."

"Welcome to our family, Ro," says King Peter. "It doesn't matter that you aren't a princess."
"Please call me Rosella, my real name," says Ro.

Queen Marissa realizes that Ro is her long-lost daughter!
Ro is a princess after all.

Color Ro's wedding dress!

The princesses finally get to be flower girls at
Ro's wedding!

Ro's animal family gets ready for the wedding, too!

Can you find 5 differences between this page and the opposite page? Circle them.

ANSWER: On this page, Tallulah's tail is missing; the curtain is missing; Tika's toes are missing from her back foot; Tika's crown is missing; and the stripes on Sagi's tail are missing.

One big happy family!